MORE SPECIAL OFFERS
FOR MR MEN AND LITTLE MISS READERS

In every Mr Men and Little Miss ▌▌▌▌▌▌▌▌▌▌▌▌▌▌▌ Men
sticker and activity books, you will find a special token. and we
will send you a gift of your choice

Choose either a <u>Mr Men</u> or <u>Little Miss</u> poster, **or** a Mr Men or Little Miss
double sided full colour bedroom door hanger.

Return this page **with six tokens per gift required** to:
     Marketing Dept., MM / LM, World International Ltd.,
     PO Box 7, Manchester, M19 2HD

Your name:_____ Age: _____

Address: _____

_____

_____Postcode: _____

Parent / Guardian Name (Please Print)_____

Please tape a 20p coin to your request to cover part post and package cost

I enclose <u>six</u> tokens per gift, and 20p please send me:-

Posters:-	Mr Men Poster ☐	Little Miss Poster ☐
Door Hangers -	Mr Nosey / Muddle ☐	Mr Greedy / Lazy ☐
	Mr Tickle / Grumpy ☐	Mr Slow / Busy ☐
	Mr Messy / Quiet ☐	Mr Perfect / Forgetful ☐
	L Miss Fun / Late ☐	L Miss Helpful / Tidy ☐
	L Miss Busy / Brainy ☐	L Miss Star / Fun ☐

Please Tick Appropriate Box

20p

Stick 20p here please

We may occasionally wish to advise you of other Mr Men gifts. ☐
If you would rather we didn't please tick this box

— 100 mm —

250 mm

ENTRANCE FEE
3 SAUSAGES

MR. GREEDY

Collect six of these tokens
You will find one inside every
Mr Men and Little Miss book
which has this special offer.

1
TOKEN

Offer open to residents of UK, Channel Isles and Ireland only

Mr Men and Little Miss Library Presentation Boxes

In response to the many thousands of requests for the above, we are delighted to advise that these are now available direct from ourselves, for only **£4.99** (inc VAT) plus 50p p&p.
The full colour boxes accommodate each complete library. They have an integral carrying handle as well as a neat stay closed fastener.
Please do not send cash in the post. Cheques should be made payable to **World International Ltd. for the sum of £5.49** (inc p&p) per box.

Please note books are not included.

Please return this page with your cheque, stating below which presentation box you would like, to:-
**Mr Men Office, World International
PO Box 7, Manchester, M19 2HD**

Your name:_____

Address: _____

_____

_____Postcode: _____

Name of Parent/Guardian (please print):_____

Signature:_____

I enclose a cheque for £_____ made payable to World International Ltd.,

Please send me a Mr Men Presentation Box ☐

Little Miss Presentation Box ☐ *(please tick or write in quantity) and allow 28 days for delivery*

Thank you

Offer applies to UK, Eire & Channel Isles only

little Miss Somersault

by Roger Hargreaves

WORLD INTERNATIONAL

Little Miss Somersault is the sort of person who doesn't just go out for a walk.

Oh no, not Little Miss Somersault.

She is too full of energy for that.

Rather than walking everywhere, she cartwheels everywhere!

She doesn't just walk through her front door.

That would be too easy.

She built a house where she could climb over the roof first!

Little Miss Somersault doesn't just sit in a chair.

She balances on the back of it.

Little Miss Somersault doesn't walk around things.

She jumps right over them!

And rather than answer the telephone
like you or I might, she …

… well, just look at her!

The other day, when she was cartwheeling past
Mr Worry's house, he called out to her.
"There's a leaf on my roof. Please could
you get it for me?" he asked.

Mr Worry had spent the whole morning worrying
that the leaf might make his roof fall in!

"I have a long ladder," he added.

Little Miss Somersault said, "I don't need a ladder."
And, quick as a flash, she climbed on top of
Mr Worry's house and got the leaf off.

A little further down the lane,
Little Miss Somersault came to
Mr Skinny's house.

Mr Skinny was at the top of a ladder,
painting his roof.

Unfortunately, Mr Bump came around the corner and walked under the ladder.

Or rather, he tried to walk under the ladder, but being Mr Bump he walked straight into it.

BUMP!

And you can see what happened!

Little Miss Somersault had seen it all happen.

And without a thought for the ladder lying on
the ground, she climbed to the top of
Mr Skinny's house and carried him
safely to the ground,
under her arm.

He wasn't very heavy!

By the next morning, everybody had heard
about Little Miss Somersault's daring deeds.

The phone rang. It was Mr Uppity.
"There's an umbrella stuck in my chimney.
I hear you're good at climbing on to roofs.
I'll expect you here in five minutes!"

Mr Uppity's house is one of the biggest
houses you will ever have seen.

"To climb to the top of Mr Uppity's house
would be a real challenge," said
Little Miss Somersault.

It took no time at all for Little Miss Somersault
to climb on to Mr Uppity's roof.

"That was easy," she said, as she
balanced on a chimney pot.

Then she looked down at the ground, far below her.

That was the last thing she should have done.
Little Miss Somersault suddenly felt dizzy.
Her knees began to tremble.
Everything began to spin round and round.

Little Miss Somersault had discovered she
was afraid of heights!

Luckily, Mr Tickle happened to be passing.

He stretched out one of his
extraordinarily long arms.

Do you think he wanted to tickle
Little Miss Somersault?

Of course he did!

But not before he had brought her back
safely down to the ground.

"Stop it!" laughed Little Miss Somersault.
"I promise I won't do anything so foolish again!"

And off went Mr Tickle to look for
somebody else to tickle.

That evening, Little Miss Somersault
was sitting, that's right, sitting, in her
armchair.

Suddenly the telephone rang.

"My hat has blown off," said a voice at the
other end. "And it's landed on the roof of
my house. Could you …"

Little Miss Somersault's face turned pale.

"Who is this?" she asked, in a trembling voice.

"It's Mr Small," said Mr Small.

Little Miss Somersault breathed a
huge sigh of relief.

"I'll be there in five minutes!" she said.

And off she somersaulted!